Fight!

"You little twerp!" Dennis screamed at Jimmy Underwood. "I'd like to bash you once and for all and put you out of your misery."

Tears ran down Jimmy's face. "They made me tell! I didn't want to!" he cried.

Dennis threw him down with disgust. "You all make me sick. I'm going to pay you back for telling on me. All of you!" And with that he stormed off.

"Oh, my gosh!" Elizabeth said as she and Amy scrambled to help the boys. "That was horrible."

Jimmy crouched by the side of the pavement, crying. "He's going to kill me. I know he is," he kept saying.

"Look, Jimmy, we're all in this together," Ken said.

Elizabeth felt absolutely awful about insisting on telling Mr. Bowman. They would have to think of something themselves next time. Something that would make Dennis leave them alone once and for all. . . .

Bantam Skylark Books in the SWEET VALLEY TWINS series
Ask your bookseller for the books you have missed.

SWEET VALLEY TWINS

The Bully

◇

Written by
Jamie Suzanne

Created by
FRANCINE PASCAL

A BANTAM SKYLARK BOOK®
TORONTO · NEW YORK · LONDON · SYDNEY · AUCKLAND

THE BULLY
A Bantam Skylark Book / May 1988

Sweet Valley High® and Sweet Valley Twins are
trademarks of Francine Pascal.

Conceived by Francine Pascal.

Produced by Daniel Weiss Associates, Inc.
27 West 20th Street
New York, NY 10011

Cover art by James Mathewuse.

Skylark Books is a registered trademark of Bantam Books.
Registered in U.S. Patent and Trademark Office and elsewhere.

"Song of the Open Road" from VERSES FROM 1929 ON by
Ogden Nash. Copyright 1932 by Ogden Nash. First appeared in
The New Yorker. By permission of Little, Brown and Company.

ISBN 0-553-15595-4

Published simultaneously in the United States and Canada

Bantam Books are published by Bantam Books, a division of Bantam
Doubleday Dell Publishing Group, Inc. Its trademark, consisting of the
words "Bantam Books" and the portrayal of a rooster, is Registered in
U.S. Patent and Trademark Office and in other countries. Marca Regis-
trada. Bantam Books, 666 Fifth Avenue, New York, New York 10103.

PRINTED IN THE UNITED STATES OF AMERICA

O   0 9 8 7 6 5 4 3 2 1

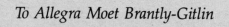

To Allegra Moet Brantly-Gitlin

One

◇

"Listen up, you guys!" Jessica Wakefield announced, tossing back her shoulder-length blond hair. She was sitting in the lunchroom on Tuesday afternoon with Ellen Riteman, Lila Fowler, and Janet Howell, fellow members of the Unicorn Club, the exclusive club the girls had formed at Sweet Valley Middle School. They called themselves Unicorns because, like the mythical creatures, they considered themselves special. Jessica loved being a member of the club and wanted to make sure it remained small. Lately a lot of sixth-grade girls had been asking to join, and Jessica was feeling a little uneasy. After all, not just *anyone* could be a Unicorn.

"Grace Oliver wants to join the club," Jessica told the others in a hushed voice. "We've talked about this before, and now I think it's time to make a new policy. No one can be admitted to the club without going through initiation rites." Jessica's blue-green eyes twinkled mischievously. She didn't mind Grace Oliver. In fact, she thought Grace would make a good club member. She just didn't want the club to lose its exclusive quality.

"Initiation rites?" Ellen Riteman repeated. "You mean like the pledge tasks we used to make new members perform?"

Before Jessica was allowed to join the club, she had to perform all sorts of daring tasks. She even had to send some girls into the boys' room. But since then, the Unicorns had simply voted on new members without any other requirements. "Can't we just vote on it and let her join?" Ellen asked.

Now it was Lila's turn to look impatient. "Come on, Ellen," she said haughtily. "Jessica is right. The whole point of having an exclusive club is that it's hard to get in. If we don't go back to initiations again, we won't be special anymore!"

Lila Fowler was the only child of one of the wealthier men in Sweet Valley, and she was used to getting her way. "OK," Ellen said, knowing she was outnumbered. "What sort of initiation rites are you talking about?"

"Well, I have some ideas," Jessica said. "Grace is in your English class. I'll talk to her before class and tell her she has to get up while Mr. Bowman is talking and recite a poem. Then you can report back and let us know whether or not she really did it."

Ellen looked doubtful. Mr. Bowman was a good teacher, but he didn't put up with nonsense. "Come on, you guys," Ellen began. "Do you really think—" But one look from Jessica and Lila made Ellen back down. She didn't feel entirely happy about this initiation business. But she knew that when Jessica had a plan, there just wasn't any way to stop her!

Jessica and Lila went off to find Grace, and Ellen went on to her English class.

Elizabeth Wakefield, Jessica's identical twin, skipped down the hall on her way to Mr. Bowman's English class. English was her favorite subject, and she always worked particularly hard on her compositions. She wanted to be a writer more than anything, and she was hoping that her experience as a staff member of *The Sweet Valley Sixers*, the sixth-grade newspaper, would give her a head start.

Elizabeth was looking forward to English class

even more than usual on this particular day. It was the day they would be reading aloud the stories they had written. She was proud of hers, about a boy who lived entirely in an imaginary world.

"Hello, Mr. Bowman." Elizabeth greeted her English teacher as she entered the classroom with her best friend, Amy Sutton.

"Oh, no!" Amy gasped as they passed his desk. "Look what Mr. Bowman is wearing today."

Elizabeth smiled. Mr. Bowman was famous for wearing colors and patterns that clashed. Today he had on a striped shirt and a paisley tie. Elizabeth didn't care much about his zany dress habits, though. He was a great teacher and that was what mattered to her.

She slipped into her seat and noticed that she was sitting beside a very nervous-looking Grace Oliver. Usually the brown-haired girl was very quiet and calm in class. Elizabeth couldn't help wondering what might be wrong. When Mr. Bowman began to talk, Grace unexpectedly stood up and blurted out a short poem:

"I think that I shall never see
A billboard lovely as a tree.
Indeed, unless the billboards fall
I'll never see a tree at all."

All the kids in the classroom turned around in their seats and craned their necks to look at Grace. Somebody snickered and Mr. Bowman cleared his throat. "Pardon me, Grace," he said pleasantly. "Would you like to continue?"

Grace was beet red by now. "No," she said in a small voice.

All the kids continued to stare except Ellen Riteman, who looked straight ahead, her cheeks pink.

"That poem is by Ogden Nash, one of my favorites," Mr. Bowman said, looking at Grace with curiosity. "Did something I said remind you of it?"

"No," Grace said miserably. "I . . . uh, I just said it because . . . uh . . . because I wanted to."

"I see," Mr. Bowman said. "Well, the next time you feel the urge to recite a poem, please check with me first."

Elizabeth and Amy exchanged puzzled looks. Elizabeth was just about to make a comment to her friend when she felt a light tap on her shoulder. Then Ken Matthews, who sat behind her, handed her a neatly folded piece of paper.

"Dear Elizabeth," the note read. "A group of us are holding a summit conference this afternoon to talk about Dennis Cookman. This is an emergency! Can you come? We're meeting at the lot behind Mr. Larson's house right after school. We really want you to be there. Bring anyone else who you think can help."

Elizabeth read the note quickly and frowned. She nodded once to Ken to show him she could come, folded the note, and slipped it inside her notebook.

She had been hearing a lot about Dennis Cookman lately. She wondered what had happened.

Dennis was in the seventh grade and had no friends. For some reason he liked hanging around the sixth-graders, especially the smaller guys like Ken Matthews and Jimmy Underwood. Hanging around wasn't exactly the right term though. He actually liked to pick on the smaller kids, both girls and boys, and lately he had been doing it more often.

When the bell rang, Elizabeth gathered her books together. "We need your help," Ken said, walking alongside her. "Cookman has been picking on Jimmy all week long. We want to do something to get even, but we don't know what."

Elizabeth always liked helping out. It really meant a lot to her that kids in her class trusted her judgment. "You can count on me to be at the meeting. I just hope I'll be able to help," she said quietly.

Jessica and Lila were standing outside the classroom as Elizabeth walked out behind Ken and Grace. "How'd it go?" Lila asked Grace.

Grace looked mortified. "I felt so silly, but I did it," she said.

Elizabeth stopped short. "Jessica, did *you* have something to do with that?" she demanded. She should have guessed that where there was trouble, Jessica couldn't be far behind!

Jessica tossed her hair back over her shoulders. "This is a private Unicorn matter, Lizzie. Come on, you guys," she said, steering Grace and Ellen away with her and Lila.

Elizabeth looked after her sister in amazement. "I don't believe her!" she cried. "How does she get away with doing things like that?"

Amy sighed. "You two sure are different."

Elizabeth knew her friend was right. As far as looks went, she and Jessica were mirror images. They both had long blond hair and blue-green eyes. Elizabeth was four minutes older than Jessica, and they always joked about her being the big sister. But, in fact, Elizabeth often did feel much older than her twin. She couldn't believe her own sister had put poor Grace up to a stunt like that. She was determined to tell Jessica what she thought of such behavior!

"Look," Amy said, interrupting Elizabeth's thoughts. "Here comes that bully Dennis Cookman!"

Elizabeth shuddered. Dennis was lumbering down the hall toward them. Everything about him was larger than life—his hands, his arms, even his big grin. He had short brown hair, a round face, and narrow slits for eyes.

"He looks like a bulldog," Amy whispered.

"Ssshhh," Elizabeth whispered back. "He might hear you!"

"Out of my way!" Dennis thundered as he careened straight toward them.

Elizabeth and Amy jumped aside to let the big seventh-grader pass them.

"Wow," Amy said. "I wouldn't want to be on his bad side. Would you?"

Elizabeth shook her head. She knew a lot of kids who had gotten on Dennis's bad side for no reason at all. Ken was right. Dennis *was* getting out of hand. It was time for them to do something.

The question was, what?

"You did a good job," Jessica said to Grace. "The thing is, you have to realize that being a Unicorn is very special. If we were to let you in right now, it wouldn't be fair to the other Unicorns." She winked at Lila. "So we're going to have you do a few more things."

Grace looked nervous. "Nothing too hard, OK? I'm really not good at stuff like that." She wet her lips. "Mr. Bowman looked pretty mad at me."

"Oh, he'll forget all about it by tomorrow," Jessica said airily, waving her hand. "We'll let you know then what your next task will be."

She and Lila watched Grace walk down the hall. "I don't know, Jess," Lila said with a frown. "Do you really think Grace will survive another task?"

"It depends," Jessica said. She was about to say more when she saw Dennis Cookman walking toward them, his face set in a horrible expression as he stormed down the hallway. "Uh-oh," she said under her breath. "Here comes disaster with a capital D."

Lila's brown eyes widened. She didn't scare easily, but she was definitely terrified now. Dennis had forced her to give him a good part of her allowance the week before and ever since then she'd been avoiding him like the plague.

"Hey, Fowler!" Dennis bellowed, coming closer.

Lila turned white as a ghost, edging behind Jessica. "Don't let him hit me, Jess," she said fearfully.

Jessica looked at her friend. "It's not going to help if you act scared, you know."

"Oh, yeah? *You* try dealing with him," Lila snapped. "It's easy for you to talk. You haven't had a run-in with him."

Jessica stood in front of Lila, crossed her arms, and glared at Dennis. Even if she *was* afraid of Dennis Cookman, she wasn't going to let it show.

"Get out of my way," Dennis growled. "I want to talk to *her*." He pointed at Lila menacingly.

Jessica took a deep breath. "What are you going to do if I don't move?" she asked him, trying hard to sound brave.

Dennis stared at Jessica, his face turning red, and he repeated gruffly, "I said, get—out—of—my—way." With each word he moved closer until he was almost touching Jessica, his eyes bulging.

Jessica gulped. "OK, OK," she said, jumping to one side.

"Fowler," Dennis growled. "Gimme ten bucks or I'm going to make you sorry."

Lila shot Jessica a desperate look as she handed Dennis a ten-dollar bill. "That's twenty-five dollars in the past two weeks," she whispered to Jessica after he disappeared with her money. "What am I going to do?"

Jessica shook her head. "That boy is worse than horrible. He's awful." She shuddered. "I really thought he was going to hit me."

Lila nodded. "Yeah, well, it wouldn't be the first time. He beat up Jimmy Underwood yesterday. He gave him a black eye and told him if he tattled, he'd punch the other eye. Jimmy's scared to death his parents will find out the truth, and then Dennis will turn him to mush."

Jessica's eyes flashed. "Dennis needs a taste of his own medicine," she declared. "Just watching him walk down the hall like he owns this place gives me the creeps."

"Well," Lila said, "if you want to help do something about it, a bunch of kids are meeting over at Larson's lot later. Ken and Jimmy are holding a council to figure out what to do."

Jessica's eyes brightened. "That's great," she said. "Let's join them. I bet you and I can come up with some kind of plan for putting that bully in his place!"

It didn't take much urging. Lila was as eager to go to the meeting as the rest of the kids in her class.

Two

◇

Elizabeth had recently started a new art class, and unfortunately, Dennis Cookman was also in it. Most of the kids in the class were sixth-graders, but a few seventh-graders had been assigned to it because of scheduling problems. Dennis had transferred into the class two weeks ago. No one knew exactly why, but there'd been a rumor that he'd gotten kicked out of his gym class after he beat up a seventh-grader during a volleyball game. Elizabeth didn't know whether or not that was true, but she did know that Dennis had done nothing but disrupt the class since he arrived.

At first all he did was sit in the corner and sulk.

When Mrs. Webster tried to encourage him to join in on the class projects, he just sneered. "I don't feel like it," he replied. Mrs. Webster, who was one of the nicest and kindest teachers in the whole middle school, seemed to be at a loss. Nobody knew what to do with Dennis.

That day when Elizabeth got to art class she paid particular attention to Dennis. She was wondering what new disaster had come up to make Ken and Jimmy call an emergency meeting. Dennis was perched on a stool near the center table, his arms folded sullenly across his chest. He was glaring at the mural that Olivia Davidson and Sarah Thomas were painting.

"That's one of the worst-looking murals I've ever seen," he said, leaning forward and poking at the edge of the painting with a dirty finger.

"Dennis!" Olivia cried. "Don't touch it! We've been working hard on this. We're going to enter it in the Art Fair."

Elizabeth came over to inspect the mural. The whole class had been working on projects for the upcoming Art Fair, but Olivia and Sarah had really knocked themselves out. "Olivia, this is wonderful!" Elizabeth exclaimed, patting her friend on the shoulder. Olivia was one of the best artists at school. She had won many prizes for her creations. The mural she had designed was a watercolor of the beach and the ocean. There were lovely boats in the harbor and the color of the sea was a perfect blend of greens and blues. "I'll bet you're going to win first prize in the fair," Elizabeth said.

Dennis leaned forward on his stool. "You're never gonna win anything with this stupid mural," he announced.

Elizabeth glared at Dennis. She couldn't believe how mean he looked. He was almost a foot taller than the tallest boy in the sixth grade, Aaron Dallas, and with his bulky frame, short light brown hair, and beady eyes he looked almost like a monster. Elizabeth swallowed hard. She didn't like Dennis at all, and she was determined to stick up for Olivia. "Nobody asked you," she said, looking straight into Dennis's brown eyes.

He stared back at her, his eyes narrowing. Half-snarling, half-growling, he said, "You just mind your own business, Miss Goody-goody Wakefield." Elizabeth tried to control her fear, and she kept her head held high as she walked over to her own table. She even managed to give Olivia a little wink. Soon Mrs. Webster came over to give her some advice on the charcoal drawing she was working on, and before long Elizabeth was so engrossed in the project that she forgot all about Dennis.

She was just about to return to the center table to see how the mural was going when Sarah Thomas came over, her face red. "Elizabeth, you've got to come help us."

Elizabeth followed Sarah over to where Olivia was stooping over a tiny section of the mural. She was trying to outline the largest sailboat, but Dennis kept kicking the table with his hiking boots.

"Dennis Cookman, cut that out right now!" Elizabeth said loudly.

"Cut what out?" Dennis snarled, kicking the table extra hard.

"Oh, no!" Olivia cried as spatters of black paint shot over the mural. "Dennis, look what you made me do!" Her eyes were indignant and tearful. "Now the mural is wrecked!"

"It stank anyway," Dennis said, climbing down from his stool and wandering off as if nothing had happened. Elizabeth put her arm around Olivia, who began sobbing uncontrollably.

"Don't worry," Elizabeth comforted her. "We'll dab up the paint with a paper towel. It isn't ruined at all!"

But Olivia was inconsolable, and Elizabeth didn't blame her. One thing was for certain. Once and for all, someone had to do something about the school bully, and that was all there was to it!

* * *

"I hate this place," Amy complained to Elizabeth as they wheeled their bikes across Larson's lot. It was a warm, sunny afternoon, and the girls had tied their jackets around their waists. The tall weeds scratched their legs as they walked.

"I know what you mean," Elizabeth said, looking around the empty lot with a frown. "It's OK now, but sometimes when we drive past here at night, you can see all kinds of creepy shadows over near Dead Man's Cave."

Amy shuddered. Dead Man's Cave was what all the kids at school called the big cavernlike opening at the far end of the lot, back near the woods. Elizabeth had heard all sorts of scary stories about it. Jimmy Underwood said he saw a ghost there one Halloween, and some kids swore that there were skeletons way in the back of the cave. The parents didn't like it either. They all thought that the town should fence off the lot and forbid trespassing. But nothing had been done yet, and it was still a favorite meeting place.

"There they are!" Elizabeth said, pointing to Ken and Jimmy. She and Amy propped their bikes up against a tree and hurried across the lot to join the others.

"What happened to you?" Amy gasped, crouching down beside Jimmy to study his eye.

"Cookman punched me," Jimmy said miserably. "I can barely see."

Elizabeth's heart went out to him. Jimmy was the smallest boy in school. He was even shorter than Ken Matthews. Everyone teased him about his size, but he was well liked and protected by the bigger guys, especially Aaron Dallas.

"Did you tell your parents?" Elizabeth asked, crouching down to examine Jimmy's eye.

Jimmy shook his head. "No," he said miserably. "He told me if I told anyone, I'd never be able to talk again. So I told my parents I bruised my eye in gym class," he concluded, hanging his head.

"We've got to get back at Dennis," Ken declared, swinging his fists in the air. "We can't let him bully us this way anymore."

"Look," Amy said, turning toward Elizabeth. "Here comes Jessica. And she's got Ellen and Lila with her."

Elizabeth was surprised. She wouldn't have guessed that Jessica cared that much about her fellow classmates. But as soon as Lila marched up, eyes flashing, she knew something had happened.

"Are you guys trying to think of some way to

get back at Dennis?" Lila asked. "Because I want to be a part of it. He's bullied me into giving him twenty-five dollars already." Lila looked furious. "At this rate I'll turn into a pauper!"

"Hey!" Aaron Dallas called across the field. "Wait up, you guys!" Aaron, one of the most popular sixth-graders, was hurrying over to join the group.

Jimmy pushed nervously at his glasses, which had been broken in his scuffle with Dennis. They were now held together with masking tape. "I think we need to scare him back—make him see what it feels like," he said.

"Yeah, but how?" Ken asked. "He's way too tough for any of us to scare. He must outweigh all of us put together. What can we do?"

"I don't know," Jimmy said. He looked across the vacant lot. "Tie him up and throw him into Dead Man's Cave," he suggested. Everyone laughed nervously. The cave wasn't really a joke—not even in the daylight.

Jessica spread her jacket out on the ground to keep her jeans clean. "Elizabeth, isn't that Steven? What's he doing here?" she asked.

The twins' older brother, Steven, was walking home from Sweet Valley High School, where he was a ninth-grader. As soon as he spotted the twins in the group, he sauntered over with a curious look on his face.

Steven Wakefield was fourteen going on obnoxious, according to the twins. He gave his sisters a hard time as often as he could. Plus, he seemed to think that being fourteen made him a complete authority on everything.

"What's going on?" he asked the group, which now included Lila, Ellen, Amy, the twins, Ken, Jimmy, and Aaron. "Looks like serious business. Are you guys planning a cookout in Dead Man's Cave?"

The girls shuddered.

Jessica looked at her brother indignantly. "We happen to be having an important meeting, for your information. It's about Dennis Cookman, the biggest bully in the middle school."

Steven laughed. "So it's a meeting. Kind of official, isn't it? Couldn't you just talk about it at school?"

Aaron and Ken both knew Steven from his basketball reputation, and they admired him. "It isn't like that, Steven," Aaron said seriously. "We've got to protect Jimmy. Look at what Dennis Cookman did to Jimmy's eye. He's got all the sixth-graders terrified. We can't talk about it at school. That's why we called a meeting out here."

Steven seemed more interested now that Aaron had explained the situation. "Hey, that's some shiner," he said to Jimmy. "Dennis did that?"

Jimmy nodded unhappily.

"So why didn't you just tell on him?" Steven asked matter of-factly. "No one's going to let Dennis get away with this kind of stuff for long—not if you tell someone about it."

"Sure—and then he'll punch out my other eye!" Jimmy cried, wincing. "Besides," he added, "I'm not a tattletale."

"You don't know what he's like," Lila told Steven. "He actually got twenty-five dollars away from me in the last two weeks. He's gruesome."

"Yeah, and he made Peter DeHaven drink muddy water last week," Jessica chimed in.

"And today he purposely wrecked Olivia Davidson and Sarah Thomas's mural in art class," Elizabeth added.

"Wait a minute," Steven said, looking from one face to the next. "I don't get it. This guy Dennis has been terrorizing you and you haven't even told anyone about it?"

"Who are we supposed to tell?" Ken asked. "Jimmy's right—we can't tattle. It'll only make it worse. We need to find a way to deal with him ourselves."

Steven looked exasperated. "You guys are nuts," he said, starting to walk off. He shook his head and turned to face the group again. "You're not going to get back at Cookman by holding meetings. If you're really serious, you're going to have to either tell someone what he's doing or you're going to have to gang up on him."

Everyone stared after Steven in silence as he walked away.

"He's right," Ken said quietly. "We sure haven't been able to think of anything that's worked. Maybe we should tell one of the teachers. Mr. Bowman, maybe."

"But Dennis will kill me," Jimmy piped up in a shaky voice.

This time, no one was listening to Jimmy. They were all hoping Steven was right. Once they told someone, maybe their troubles would be over.

Three

◇

As Elizabeth and Amy walked to school the next day, they discussed the problem of Dennis Cookman again. "My brother really thinks we're jerks," Elizabeth said with a sigh. "You should've heard him at dinner last night, going on and on about how babyish we're being. The worst thing was that he got my parents going, too. My dad thinks if we don't tell the teachers about Dennis, we're—" She frowned. "How did he put it? We're encouraging the bullying, that's what he said."

Amy groaned. "Yeah, but are your father and Steven going to be there when Dennis finds out someone tattled? It's easy for them to talk. They're not the ones who are going to get pulverized!"

"Still," Elizabeth said, shifting her books, "I kind of think they're right. We have to do *something*, Amy. I mean, it's obvious that things can't go on this way!"

Amy nodded, but Elizabeth could tell her mind was on something else. "Elizabeth," Amy said, "has Jessica said anything to you about Grace Oliver joining the Unicorns?"

"No. She knows I don't like talking about the Unicorns," Elizabeth said. "Why?"

"I just wondered. Grace called me last night sounding really upset. She said she needed to borrow my social studies homework—that it was really urgent and she couldn't say why. But she said it had to do with the Unicorns."

Elizabeth remembered then what had happened in Mr. Bowman's class. "I'd better talk to Jessica," she said. "I hope those girls aren't putting Grace through some sort of stupid initiation! Remember what they wanted me to do when Jessica insisted that I join? They wanted me to put shaving cream on Lois Waller's ice-cream sundae. I thought they would have stopped doing that sort of stuff by now."

"Well, I hate to say it, but I don't think they have. Grace said she needed to get six people's homework papers by this morning. Doesn't that sound like the kind of crazy thing your sister would dream up?"

Elizabeth frowned. She couldn't help defending Jessica, even though she knew Amy was probably right. "I know she goes a little far sometimes with the Unicorn business, and maybe she even made Grace recite that poem. But I'm sure she wouldn't make Grace take people's *homework*."

Amy didn't say anything. She knew how protective Elizabeth could be of her twin, but she had a hunch this time Elizabeth didn't really believe what she was saying.

The girls were almost at the entrance to the school now, and Amy grabbed Elizabeth's arm. "Oh, no," she whispered. "Look over there!"

Elizabeth looked across to where Amy was pointing. At the far end of the parking lot she saw Dennis Cookman standing over Jimmy Underwood. Dennis's back was to the girls, but they could see that Jimmy was absolutely terrified.

"Come on!" Elizabeth exclaimed, tugging at her friend's arm. "We've got to get to Jimmy before Dennis gives him another black eye!"

Amy thought fast. "Dennis!" she called.

"Somebody over there was just talking about you behind your back. I could have sworn I heard one of those guys over there say that you were a wimp."

Dennis squinted at the group of eighth-graders Amy pointed to. He looked like he didn't know whether or not to believe her. Then he turned to Jimmy, glowering. "Next time when I ask you for something, you'd better give it to me. Understand?" With that he stomped off toward the group of boys.

"What did he want you to give him?" Elizabeth asked, putting her arm around Jimmy, who was trembling violently.

Jimmy's eyes were filled with tears, but he was trying desperately to gain control of himself. He didn't want to seem like a baby in front of Elizabeth and Amy. "He . . . he took my pocket calculator, that's all," he said, standing up straighter. "No big deal."

Elizabeth and Amy exchanged glances. Jimmy was white as a ghost and still trembling, and it was obvious that Dennis had scared him to death.

"This is getting out of hand," Elizabeth said. "Jimmy, meet me in Mr. Bowman's class as soon as the bell rings for lunch. If you see Ken or Aaron, tell them to come, too."

"Why?" Jimmy demanded, his voice high. "What are you going to do?"

"I'm going to tell Mr. Bowman," Elizabeth said. "And I want you to be there with me."

Mr. Bowman, who was wearing a polka-dot bow tie and a plaid shirt, paced back and forth behind his desk. He listened closely as Elizabeth and Ken described Dennis Cookman's reign of terror. Jimmy sat at one of the desks in the front, listening quietly and looking defeated. When the two were done with their account, Mr. Bowman turned to Jimmy.

"Is all this true, Jimmy? Did Dennis Cookman really give you that black eye?"

Jimmy nodded. "But if you tell him who told you, he's going to make my whole body black and blue," he stammered.

Mr. Bowman stopped pacing. "Hmm," he said at last. "I guess that means that I'm the only teacher you've told about this."

"Yes, that's true," Elizabeth said. "We didn't want to snitch. But it seems like things are getting out of hand. After he ruined Olivia's mural yesterday . . . and then this morning, taking Jimmy's calculator . . . it just didn't seem like there was a way to stop him."

Mr. Bowman looked thoughtful. "I appreciate what you're telling me. I want you all to know you

have my sympathy. I'll speak to Dennis this afternoon, and I assure you that there will be a change in
his behavior at once."

"Sure," Jimmy muttered under his breath. "I'll
bet."

Elizabeth already felt better. Steven and Mr.
Wakefield were right—talking to someone in authority was the best way to handle this situation.

"One final thing," Mr. Bowman added. "You
know, in my experience, when someone behaves
this way, it's usually a signal that something else is
wrong. If Dennis weren't so insecure, he wouldn't
have to bully you kids this way."

"He sure didn't look insecure when he was giving me a black eye," Jimmy said.

Elizabeth put a reassuring hand on Jimmy's
arm. She knew Mr. Bowman was trying to help, and
though she didn't blame Jimmy for being scared, she
didn't want to seem unappreciative. "Thanks, Mr.
Bowman," she said gratefully. "We're really glad
you're going to talk to Dennis."

Mr. Bowman nodded, tapping the ruler on his
desk. "I'm going to go to the office right away and
have him paged. Don't worry, Jimmy," he added,
patting the small boy on the shoulder. "I intend to let
Dennis know exactly what the consequences of his
behavior might be. If he doesn't shape up at once, he

risks being put on probation—and possibly being asked to leave school for good."

Jimmy bit his lip nervously as he walked away with Ken and Elizabeth. "I still don't believe this will make Dennis change," he muttered to Elizabeth. "What if he thinks I tattled?"

Elizabeth laughed lightly and squeezed Jimmy's arm. "Stop worrying," she said. She was sure that once Mr. Bowman talked to Dennis, everything would go back to normal.

"Anyone want to watch the Little League game in the park?" Aaron asked, wheeling his bike over to where Ken, Amy, Elizabeth, and Jimmy were standing. School had just let out and everyone was trying to decide what to do.

"Sounds good to me," Ken said. "You guys want to come?"

"Sure," Elizabeth said. She had planned to do some work on the paper, but it was too nice a day to stay inside. Soon they were all walking in the direction of the park, Aaron wheeling his bike alongside them.

"Hey," Jimmy said suddenly, his voice unnaturally high. "Do you guys see what I see?" He pointed to the cluster of bushes in front of them. A huge shadow was cast from behind the bushes. Elizabeth raised her eyes and immediately recognized the unmistakable form of Dennis Cookman.

"Just act normal," Ken said in a low voice. "There's five of us and only one of him."

Jimmy was trembling like a leaf, but he kept up with the others.

Dennis strolled out to the middle of the sidewalk and turned to face them. "Well, what do you know," he said. "If it isn't the little tattletales out for a walk. Bowman gave me his little lecture today. You guys think you're so smart. Gonna get me put on probation . . . or maybe even suspended? Is that the plan?"

"Cut it out, Dennis," Aaron said. "Move over and let us pass."

"Move over," Dennis imitated in a mocking voice. He stared at Aaron. "Is that what you said? You gonna go tell *Mr. Bowman* if I don't?"

"Dennis," Ken began in a reasonable voice, "we didn't want to say anything, but—"

Dennis didn't let him finish. With one swift pounce he leapt on top of Ken, knocking him down on the pavement. Aaron promptly dropped his bike and climbed on Dennis's back, punching at him from behind. Within seconds a full-scale brawl had broken out. Jimmy and the girls looked on with horror as Dennis pinned the two boys together beneath him.

"I'm going to knock you out, you dumb jerks," Dennis said. "And I'll get you, too, Jimmy Undersized! You'll be sorry you ever said a word to Mr. Bowman."

Ken and Aaron were both winded from the exertion of the struggle. Jimmy, terrified when he heard his name, had run off into the bushes, but it didn't take Dennis long to catch up to him.

"You little twerp," Dennis screamed. "I'd like to bash you once and for all and put you out of your misery."

Tears ran down Jimmy's face. "They made me tell! I didn't want to!" he cried.

Dennis threw him down with disgust. "You all make me sick. I'm going to pay you back for telling on me. All of you." With that he stormed off, leaving Ken and Aaron still struggling to get up off the sidewalk. The boys were more humiliated than hurt, though Ken had a scratch over his right eye and Aaron's hand had started to swell from punching Dennis so hard.

"Oh, my gosh," Elizabeth said as she and Amy scrambled to help the boys. "That was *horrible*."

Jimmy crouched by the side of the pavement,

crying. "He's going to kill me. I know he is," he kept saying.

"Look, Jimmy, we're all in this together," Ken said, brushing himself off and glaring at Dennis's retreating back.

"Maybe telling Mr. Bowman wasn't such a great idea," Aaron said to Elizabeth as she helped him to his feet. "Looks like we're back to the drawing board on this one, guys."

No one said anything. The Little League game in the park had been forgotten, and they were all too shocked to talk about what had just happened.

Elizabeth felt absolutely awful about telling Mr. Bowman. They would have to think of something themselves next time. Something that would make Dennis leave them alone once and for all.

"Well," Lila said, her eyes shining, "she did it, Jessica. Grace came up with six different kids' homework assignments this morning. She passed. *Now* do we vote on her and let her be a Unicorn?"

Jessica and Lila were over at Ellen's house that afternoon. Jessica wrinkled her nose. "She hasn't done anything really difficult yet," she objected. "I thought the whole point was to make becoming a Unicorn as hard as possible. All she's had to do so far is recite a poem and borrow some homework."

"What next?" Ellen said anxiously. "Jess, we don't want to make it *too* hard. We might lose her. She's not the bravest girl in the world, you know."

Jessica fiddled with her hair band. What would be something hard . . . really hard? Something to show whether or not Grace was really special enough to be a Unicorn.

Ellen got up to change the radio station. "I hate to change the subject, but did you all hear about Dennis Cookman? Some kids told on him and now he's out for revenge. Grace called me after school today and said she and her friend Beth ran into Jimmy Underwood. He said Dennis beat up Ken and Aaron on their way to the park this afternoon."

Lila looked grim. "I'd better ask Daddy to put my allowance right into the bank. It's getting awfully dangerous at school with Dennis on the loose."

"It's strange. Dennis doesn't have one single friend," Ellen observed, sitting down again. "You never see him *talking* to anyone at school."

Everyone was quiet for a minute.

"That's true," Jessica said suddenly, snapping her fingers.

Ellen and Lila stared at her. "What is it, Jess?" Lila asked uneasily. "She's got that look on her face— like something's up," she said to Ellen.

"I just figured out what we can ask Grace to do,

that's all," Jessica said, grinning. "It'll be . . . how can we put it . . . sort of a test of social skills. What do you say we tell Grace she has to get Dennis Cookman to eat lunch with her?"

"No way!" Lila cried.

"Jessica, that's cruel! It would be easier to ask her to spend a night on Mars," Ellen objected.

But Jessica's eyes were shining. It was a perfect test—absolutely perfect. And she had every intention of getting her way on this one!

Four

◇

Aaron paced back and forth with his hands in his jeans' pockets. "I think what Jimmy said is right. The only way to get back at Dennis is on his own terms. Scare him the way he's been scaring us."

It was Thursday afternoon, right after school, and Elizabeth, Ken, Aaron, Amy, and Jimmy were having another emergency meeting in Larson's lot. Things had been even worse at school that day. Dennis had sneaked into the locker room during Ken's gym class and had stolen his school clothes out of his locker. Ken had to wear his gymsuit all morning until his mother came with a change of clothes. Next he had gotten behind Aaron in the lunch line and had stepped on his foot as hard as he could. And when Amy had bent down over the drinking fountain to get a drink, he had purposely pushed into her so her face went right into the water.

Elizabeth's mind was miles away this afternoon. She wished Aaron and Ken could think of a better place to have these summits. As she stared across the lot to Dead Man's Cave, she thought to herself, *This place is really creepy.*

"I think we're wasting our time," Jimmy said in a small voice. "Let's face it. Dennis is ten times bigger than any of us and fifty times stronger. He's just going to keep picking on us till he gets tired of it."

"But Dennis isn't exactly a heavyweight when it comes to brains," Aaron said. "My idea is that we put our heads together and use the real advantage we've got."

Elizabeth looked doubtfully at Amy. "I don't really see how brains are going to help, Aaron," she said. "This time it seems to me like brains aren't good for much."

Aaron narrowed his eyes, thinking hard. "Try this one out. Suppose I happen to say—in front of Dennis—that I'm going to do something *really* scary, something incredibly dangerous that no one in their right mind would ever do. And then right after I say it, Ken here"—Aaron elbowed Ken—"says he's going to do it. And then *Jimmy* says he's going to do it, too. Wouldn't that shame Dennis into saying he'd do it, too?"

"I don't get it," Ken said. "What kind of scary thing are you talking about?"

Aaron smiled, jumping lightly off the log he'd been standing on. "Try this for scary," he said, his smile getting broader. "What would you all say if I told you I planned to spend the night—the whole night—in Dead Man's Cave?"

A stunned silence fell over the group. Jimmy turned white and got to his feet. "No way. I'm not going near that place. My sister said she saw a big dark shape in there last Halloween!"

"Aw, come on," Aaron said. "I'm not afraid of a bunch of stupid stories. You're not either, are you, Ken?"

Ken suddenly seemed very interested in a stick lying on the ground next to him. "Well . . . uh, Aaron, it isn't like the stories just come from one person or anything. I mean, there happens to be a lot of evidence that . . . The whole night? You mean spend the whole night in there?" Ken looked pale at the thought.

Aaron laughed. "OK, I'll stop torturing you. Come with me. I've got something to show you." He frowned. "Only you have to swear—cross your hearts and hope to die—that you won't tell anyone. My brother told me if I gave this secret away he'd take back the entire knife collection he gave me last year. You all swear?"

Everyone solemnly promised never to tell.

"Where are you taking us?" Jimmy asked as they started off across the lot.

"To the cave!" Aaron called. "Don't worry," he added. "Nothing's going to hurt you, Jimmy. And I'm going to show you the secret passageway that's going to make *us* all look like heroes, while Dennis Cookman looks like a big baby!"

Several minutes later the five of them were standing in front of the entrance to the cave. They were all quiet for a minute. The mouth of the cave was about eight feet wide, leading back, and down, under the wooded hill at the back of the lot. It was nothing but a big dark hole. And no one, as far as Elizabeth knew, had ever spent the night there. The thought made her shudder.

"My brother was playing kickball in this lot last year with some of his buddies and the ball went straight down into the cave," Aaron said. "That's how he found out about the secret passageway. Come on, I'll show you."

Amy looked apprehensively at Elizabeth. Ken shrugged, then swallowed hard. "I'll go first," he said. "Let's go, Aaron. When I come back alive, they'll all know it's OK."

Elizabeth, Amy, and Jimmy watched nervously as the two boys disappeared into the mouth of the cave. At first they could hear their voices, but then they seemed to fade.

"You're not getting me near this place in the dark, I can tell you that right now," Jimmy said as he pushed his glasses up on his nose.

"Jimmy," Elizabeth said firmly, "Aaron's trying to help you. We all have to stay together on this. If he's got a good plan, it's worth following it—to scare Dennis. Wouldn't you like to see that?"

"I guess so," Jimmy said. He stared miserably at the cave. "But—"

"Over here, you guys!" Aaron called, waving his arms wildly. Ken stood beside him in the woods up the hill. Somehow they had gotten out of the cave—from the back—and up into the woods!

"There really is a secret passageway!" Amy exclaimed.

They waited expectantly for Ken and Aaron to come back. About five minutes later they emerged—through the mouth of the cave—looking a little dirty, but triumphant.

"That's the coolest thing," Ken said. "You guys should see it. There's a big rain pipe in the cave. It's just past this first bend, and you can crawl right through the pipe out into the woods!"

Aaron brushed off his hands. "Yeah. My brother says it doesn't work, though—the angle's all wrong or something, so the rainwater comes down from the pipe into the cave." He shrugged. "Anyway, the point is, there's a way out. And the best thing is, you'd never know it, unless you crawled all the way to the back. Come on in and I'll show you."

Elizabeth, Amy, and Jimmy filed into the cave behind Aaron. It was damp and very cool inside, and Elizabeth felt shivery again. The cave ceiling wasn't very high so they had to stoop a little as they went.

"Dennis is too big to get all the way back here," Aaron called out with satisfaction. "And even if he looked, he'd probably stop when he saw this." He pointed to a wall of earth that looked like it was the back of the cave. Around a very sharp turn the cave suddenly filled with light, and Elizabeth could see the rain pipe, which was three or four feet wide and about eight feet long. Soon they were at the other end, scrambling up the hill into the woods.

"That's neat," Amy said. Even Jimmy looked impressed.

"OK," Aaron said. "So here's the plan. Tomorrow's Friday, right? We'll wait until we're all together—in front of Dennis. We'll have to find him at lunch or something. Then someone's got to mention the cave. Say something scary happened here recently—make up a story or something." Aaron was getting excited. "The next thing to do is to make a dare. Amy, maybe you can do it. Act like we're all chicken and you're disgusted with us. Dare someone to spend the whole night in the cave."

Amy's eyes shone. She liked her role so far. "Maybe I can even say I know someone who did it and I bet none of you guys would," she suggested.

"Yeah, that sounds great," Aaron said. "The thing is to make sure Dennis hears. Then comes the moment when I say I'll do it." He thought for a minute. "You know, it'll be better if just the five of us know about the secret passageway. That way everyone else will be really shocked and horrified. They won't even have to be acting."

"So the idea is that Dennis is supposed to get forced into saying he'll spend the whole night in the cave, too, right?" Elizabeth asked. "But what if he doesn't go for it?"

Aaron shook his head. "You know Dennis. He's got everyone thinking he's so tough. If we all say we'll spend the night in the cave, he's going to feel like he's got to do it, too. Especially if we all start hinting that we think he's too scared to do it."

"This is great!" Jimmy cried. "Aaron, you're a genius! This is the best plan I've ever heard in my whole life!"

Elizabeth was still thinking about the plan. "So . . . are you really going to spend the night in there?"

"No, and that's the best part," Aaron said. "People will *think* I'm spending the night there, but I really won't. I'll enter the cave with everyone watching. We'll set a time the next morning for everyone to return so they can see me come back out. But what I'll really do is go into the cave, crawl out the secret way, and walk back to my house! Then I'll come back in the morning, sneak back through the rain pipe, and come out the front of the cave when it's time." He grinned. "Easiest way I can think of to be a hero!"

Elizabeth and Amy started clapping.

"Aaron, I have to hand it to you. That's a master plan," Ken said, patting him on the back. "I think Dennis is going to be scared out of his wits."

"And we can tell all sorts of scary stories before Dennis goes in," Elizabeth added. "We'll have Dennis Cookman wishing he'd never *thought* about pushing anyone around."

Everyone laughed. They knew the plan was a good one. No one could wait for school the next day.

Five

◇

Jessica, Ellen, and Lila met Grace after science class on Friday morning. "We want to have lunch with you," Jessica said. "We had a Unicorn meeting yesterday, and we decided you've done a good job so far and we're only going to ask you to do *one* more thing."

Grace looked thrilled. "I'm so happy. I was beginning to get worried," she confessed. Lila glanced away, and Grace frowned. "It isn't anything too difficult, is it?"

"Oh, no," Jessica said reassuringly. "It's simple. And just think," she added. "If you pass this test, we can vote you in as a full-fledged Unicorn. You'll get to wear purple and attend all the meetings." Purple was the Unicorns' favorite color. In fact, Jessica had just finished dyeing most of her white socks purple to add to her Unicorn wardrobe. If Grace managed to get Dennis to eat lunch with her, maybe Jessica would even give her a pair as an initiation gift.

The bell rang. "Meet us at lunch and we'll tell you all about it," Jessica said and hurried off to math class.

At lunchtime the four girls met in a corner of the lunchroom that Jessica had renamed the Unicorner. It was the perfect place to talk in private.

"Now, don't panic," Ellen said, patting Grace on the arm. "Your pledge task sounds a lot worse than it really is."

"Yeah," Lila said, inspecting her sandwich. "Panicking never helps anyway."

Grace looked alarmed. "I thought you said this was an easy one. You did say that, Jessica, didn't you?"

Jessica took a big bite of her sandwich. "It *is* easy. It's just going to require *tact*, that's all. And, knowing you, it should be a snap."

"The suspense is killing me. What is it?" Grace demanded.

"Do you know Dennis Cookman?" Jessica asked casually.

Grace made a face. "Who doesn't? That's like asking the people in *Jaws* if they know what a shark is."

Lila and Ellen laughed, but Jessica looked solemn. "Well," she said, "we want you to get him to have lunch with you."

Grace's eyes widened. "What?" she demanded. "Get him to have lunch with me? Are you kidding?"

"Why not?" Jessica asked innocently, polishing off the rest of her sandwich. "He can't be *that* bad once you get to know him. And you don't have to be his friend or anything. Just get him to sit with you through lunch once. That's all." Jessica crumpled up her napkin. "We realize it may take a little buttering up and everything, so we're going to give you till the end of next week."

"The end of next week!" Grace wailed. "I'll *never* be able to do it," she said, sounding totally dejected. "I want to be a Unicorn, but this is just too much. Dennis Cookman is a monster. He can't even say hello without punching you out first. How in the world am I going to get him to eat lunch with me?"

Lila and Ellen looked sympathetic, but Jessica was unrelenting. "Grace, don't give up now. You've done well so far. Just get through this one last task and you're in—for life." When Grace looked unconvinced, she added, "I know it seems hard. But we all had to prove ourselves to be Unicorns. It wouldn't be fair if you didn't do the same."

"I guess so," Grace said unhappily. She was staring across the lunchroom at Dennis, who was sitting alone as usual. Today he was blowing air into lunch bags and popping them. She couldn't imagine anything more impossible than having to share a lunch hour with him. But she would just have to do it. She wanted to be a Unicorn more than anything.

"Now, remember," Jessica instructed, "this initiation is a Unicorn secret. Everyone here has to vow their silence. And, of course, Dennis can't know why you're doing this."

After they all made their pact, Jessica turned to Grace. "Good luck," she said, smiling. "You know we'll all be rooting for you."

Meanwhile, across the lunchroom, Aaron put down the carton of milk he'd been drinking and winked at Amy. That was her cue that it was time to start the "Dennis challenge."

The Fearless Five, as Aaron had started calling them, had met before lunch to rehearse. They had deliberately chosen to sit at the end of the long table where Dennis usually sat. Peter DeHaven and Caroline Pearce were at the same table. Elizabeth thought it was almost a lucky break that Caroline happened to be there. She was the biggest gossip in the whole school and she'd be sure to spread the news about their little stunt more quickly than anyone.

Dennis was sitting alone at the next table. Amy waited until she knew she had his attention. "I heard the scariest thing about Dead Man's Cave this morning," she said loudly, unwrapping her sandwich.

"What?" Ken said on cue.

"You know my cousin, the one in high school? Well, she said she and a group of her friends went there just to hang out. When it got dark, they saw dark shadows moving across the entrance to the cave." Amy paused and shuddered.

Aaron made a great show of sounding casual. "Big deal. I think all that stuff about Dead Man's Cave is just a lot of baloney."

"Oh, yeah?" Ken cut in, just as they had rehearsed. "I'll bet you wouldn't be talking that way if you'd been there."

Caroline looked horrified. "Don't even talk about that place. My sister once saw a skeleton lying inside." She grimaced. "It's disgusting."

"It's just an old hole in the ground," Aaron protested. "You're wrong, Ken. I'm not one bit scared of Dead Man's Cave."

"Prove it!" Ken demanded.

Everyone was quiet for a second. Dennis was listening intently now.

"OK," Aaron said, as if an idea had just come to him. "Would you believe I'm not scared if I say I'll spend a whole night in there—all by myself?"

Caroline covered her face with her hands. "Aaron!" she cried. "I can't believe you're saying that!"

Aaron glanced over to make sure Dennis was still listening. "Why?" he scoffed. "What's so scary about spending the night in that old place?"

Dennis couldn't contain himself anymore. "What a tough guy. I bet you'll be running home the minute it gets dark."

Aaron shrugged, cool as could be. "Why don't you come watch me if you don't believe me?" he said. "You name the night, and I'll be there."

Dennis was quiet as he studied Aaron with new interest. "You're just bluffing," he said at last. "I'm not going to waste my time waiting for someone who's not even going to show up."

"Try me," Aaron said. "Let's say tomorrow night. I'll meet you at the cave at seven o'clock. And you can just sit there and see if I don't spend the whole night in there!"

Caroline and Peter, who had been listening to

the whole thing, were genuinely horrified. The others did their best to appear as shocked as possible. Elizabeth even hammed it up a bit by trying to talk Aaron out of it, saying she thought it was a bad idea—that the cave was too dangerous.

"I'm going to do it and that's that," Aaron said at last. "We just have to get one thing straight. No one tells any grown-ups about this. 'Cause if my parents find out, they'll never let me out of the house."

"What a joke," Dennis said. "Look who's telling who not to tattle!"

Everyone was quiet for a minute as Dennis approached the table.

He didn't touch Aaron. He just looked him straight in the eye. "You're not going to spend the whole night in that cave," he snorted. "But you can count on one thing, Aaron. I'll be there to watch you make a fool of yourself!"

Elizabeth watched him stomp off before turning to give Aaron the thumbs-up sign. The challenge had gone just the way they'd hoped. Now they just had to get everything in order for tomorrow night.

Grace had been watching Dennis from across the lunchroom. She took a deep breath. The best plan was to take it slowly, she told herself. Today was

Friday. She had a whole week to get Dennis to agree to eat lunch with her. Today all she had to do was break the ice.

She followed Dennis out of the lunchroom and down the hall, telling herself that there had to be some way to get through to him. He had to have a nice streak somewhere, didn't he?

She followed him halfway down the hall and was trying to gather up the courage to speak when he suddenly swung around. Staring down at her with a malicious look on his face, he said, "What do you think you're doing, sneaking around behind me that way? Get lost, you little runt!"

Grace stared at him, stung. "I . . . I just wanted to ask you . . . uh . . ."

"I said get lost!" Dennis snapped again.

Grace backed off, her eyes filled with tears. Then she spun around and raced back down the hallway, running smack into Jessica in front of the gym.

"Grace! What's wrong?" Jessica said.

Grace wiped her eyes. "Jessica, it's impossible. There's no way Dennis is ever going to eat lunch with me. He nearly bit my head off just now when I tried to just talk to him."

Jessica looked thoughtful. "Don't give up. You just have to have a plan, Grace. Work on him a little bit each day. I know you can do it. By Friday he'll be *giving* you his lunch. I'm sure of it." Jessica really didn't want Grace to quit now. Lila and Ellen had been opposed to her initiation scheme from the very beginning. If Grace dropped out now, Jessica would never hear the end of it. She could just hear what they'd say. "I told you so! I told you so!"

Grace looked at Jessica as if she were crazy. "I don't think so, Jessica. Have you ever tried to talk to him?"

"Well, not really," Jessica admitted. "But, Grace, you're the nicest person in the world. You're bound to make him feel like being civil. If anyone can do it, you can!" *There*, she thought. *How's that for encouragement?*

Grace didn't say a thing. She couldn't agree with Jessica less. Dennis Cookman didn't look as if he would ever be nice to anyone.

Six

◇

On Saturday morning Elizabeth was awakened by wild pounding on her door. Before she could even move, Jessica marched in, already dressed, her hair tied back in a purple headband. Her eyes flashed with excitement.

"You didn't tell me Aaron Dallas is going to spend the night in Dead Man's Cave!" she cried indignantly. Jessica had spent the night at Lila's and hadn't heard the news until Caroline Pearce called up to share it. And if there was anything Jessica hated, it was being the last one to know.

Elizabeth buried her face in the pillow and groaned. "Maybe *I* should spend the night in the cave," she murmured. "That way you couldn't barge in and wake me."

Jessica ignored this. "Why didn't you tell me, Lizzie? Caroline said you were sitting right there at lunch yesterday when Aaron announced it. You could've told me," she added, insulted. "Now I'm going to have to cancel going to the movies tonight with Ellen and Janet."

"Why?" Elizabeth asked groggily.

"What do you mean, why? You expect me to miss watching Aaron spend the night in the cave?" Jessica shrieked.

Elizabeth sat up and clapped her hand over her twin's mouth. "Ssshh," she said warningly. "If Mom or Dad hears about this, no one's going to get near that cave tonight or ever. So be quiet!"

"You know," Jessica said thoughtfully, "I never would've given Aaron credit for being so brave." She bounced over to Elizabeth's mirror to inspect her reflection. "He's kind of cute, don't you think? He looks older than a lot of the other sixth-graders."

"Jessica," Elizabeth said patiently, "leave Aaron alone. He's going to have enough to think about today without you telling him you have a crush on him."

Jessica tossed back her long silky hair, still staring at herself in the mirror. "Well," she said, "I just think someone should be ready to comfort him in case he faints or something."

Elizabeth reached for her bathrobe. There was still a lot of planning to do before seven o'clock, and she wanted to get hold of Amy right away to see what she could do to help. She would have to be very careful though. There was no way that Jessica could find out about their plan. "Jessie," she said cheerfully, "Mom asked me to ask you if you'd help me clean the house this morning. She wants us to vacuum, and to dust the hallway, and—"

Jessica lost interest in her reflection at once. "Sorry, Lizzie, but I absolutely *swore* to Lila that I'd meet her at the mall in half an hour." Jessica sailed out of the bedroom, and Elizabeth grinned. That ought to insure that Jessica would stay far from home all morning. Nothing like the threat of work to make Jessica disappear!

Now Elizabeth could have some privacy to call Amy and find out what last-minute plans still needed to be worked out before the evening.

Grace looked down at the baseball mitt in her hand and sighed. "Cookman" was written in black indelible marker across the side of it. It was a strange coincidence that she was the one to find it Friday afternoon after school. It was behind the bleachers of the playing field where Grace had been watching the cheering squad. When she caught sight of it, she picked it up, thinking that she would take it to the Lost and Found. But when she saw whose name was on it, she decided to hold on to it. That way she could bring it over to Dennis's house on Saturday morning. Scary as the idea of going over to his house was, it seemed like the perfect plan. He was bound to be grateful to her for coming all the way over to his house to deliver it to him.

But now, standing on the Cookmans' front porch, Grace wished she had left the mitt in the Lost and Found after all. The thought of ringing the doorbell and having to face Dennis terrified her. *Here goes nothing*, she thought. Her heart was pounding wildly as she rang the doorbell. The inside of her mouth felt as dry as cotton.

Mrs. Cookman came to the door. "Hello," she said, smiling at Grace. "Can I help you?"

"I . . . uh, I've come to see Dennis. Is he home?" Grace asked hopefully.

Mrs. Cookman looked surprised, then she smiled. "Just a minute. I'll call him." She turned back inside. "Denny!" she called. "A friend of yours is here to see you!" The way she said *friend* made Grace feel weird.

"Who is it?" Dennis yelled downstairs, sounding just about as gruff and awful as he did at school.

"Denny, come downstairs and find out!" Mrs. Cookman called. Grace looked longingly at the sidewalk. She wished she'd never come.

"Oh," Dennis said, coming out onto the porch and staring at Grace. "It's you. What do *you* want?" Mrs. Cookman had disappeared, much to Grace's alarm. She felt better when his mother was there.

"Here," Grace said awkwardly, extending her arm and showing him the mitt. "I found this yesterday behind the bleachers. I thought you might be missing it."

Dennis took the mitt. "Yeah, it's mine. I thought someone stole it," he said. He gave her a look as though he still thought so.

"Well," Grace said, blushing, "I found it, and I brought it over. That's all." She turned and hurried down the steps, her heart pounding. Why did Dennis have to have such a mean look on his face all the time?

"Hey, wait a minute," Dennis called after her. Grace turned around, staring at him. "Is that why you were creeping around after me in the halls yesterday?"

Grace decided to nod her head yes. It made her look nicer.

"Oh," Dennis said, looking down at the mitt.

Then he jerked his head in what seemed to be a nod of thanks. He wasn't scowling, either. Grace turned and hurried off, her heart still pounding.

But she felt like she had made a little bit of progress. Maybe when she said hi to him in school on Monday he wouldn't snap her head off.

"OK, now," Elizabeth said to Aaron as they walked together toward Larson's lot. "We hid a flashlight just behind the bend—before the rain pipe. Is there anything else you think you'll need?"

"Nope," Aaron said. "I'll stay in the cave for about an hour and then slip out the back."

Elizabeth nodded. The rules they had decided on in front of Dennis were very explicit: no flashlight, and nothing but a lunch bag with some food inside it and a canteen filled with water.

It was twilight when they reached the lot. By a quarter to seven over a dozen kids had shown up to watch Aaron enter the cave. Most important, Dennis was there, looking as mean as ever and even bigger than usual in a grubby sweatshirt.

"Get over here, Dallas," Dennis cried when he saw Aaron. "I want to make sure you don't have a flashlight hidden on you somewhere." He frisked Aaron roughly but found nothing and let him go.

Aaron looked at his watch. "It's five to seven," he said. "I'll stay in Dead Man's Cave twelve hours. Who's going to be here tomorrow morning at seven to see me come out?"

Everyone cheered and hollered. Apparently everyone intended to come.

Jessica put her hand on Aaron's arm. "You can still change your mind," she said, looking uneasily at the dark cave. "You really don't have to do this, Aaron."

Aaron laughed. "I'm not scared," he said. He made a point of looking right at Dennis when he said that.

Jimmy gave Elizabeth a little nudge, then Elizabeth nudged Amy. It was a strange feeling, knowing that the five of them knew something no one else knew. Everyone else looked at Aaron with admiration, like he was some kind of hero.

"Well," Aaron said at last, stretching as if he were about to take a long nap, "here goes nothing, I guess. Anyone want to say anything to me before I go in?"

"Good luck, Aaron," Ken said solemnly, shaking his hand and trying to look scared for his sake. Of course everyone else wanted to shake Aaron's hand, too, and wish him luck.

"It's seven o'clock," Dennis growled. "Get in there if you're going!"

Aaron grinned. "I'm on my way," he said. And with that he disappeared into the dark mouth of Dead Man's Cave.

Everyone was quiet for a minute.

"Aaron?" Jessica called. "Are you . . . uh, are you OK in there?"

"Fine!" Aaron called out. "Couldn't be better. It's a little dark in here, but otherwise it isn't so bad."

"Just wait till three in the morning, when no one is out here," Dennis taunted.

"I'll get a good night's sleep, that's all," Aaron replied.

Everyone was quiet again, listening. Every once in a while a twig snapped. It was starting to get dark.

Jimmy got to his feet. "I promised my mom I'd be home by eight," he said. "I guess I'd better get going."

"Wait, I'll go with you," Caroline Pearce said, getting to her feet, too.

One by one people started to leave.

"Aaron?" Elizabeth called. "We're going now, OK? We'll be back at seven tomorrow morning."

"OK," a muffled voice called back.

"Aw," Dennis said with a look of disgust on his face, "there's no way he's going to make it through till morning. I'll bet you anything when we get back tomorrow he'll be gone."

Elizabeth and Amy winked at each other. They knew Dennis was wrong. And they had a feeling he was going to be very surprised.

Seven

◇

Elizabeth and Jessica each set their alarms for six-thirty on Sunday morning so they'd be sure to be back at Larson's lot in time to see whether or not Aaron had made it through the night. Elizabeth couldn't help enjoying the fact that her twin didn't know about the secret passageway. "I'll bet he chickened out and went home in the middle of the night," Jessica kept saying as they hopped on their bikes and quietly pedaled out of the garage. They didn't want to wake their parents or Steven. The sun was just rising as they approached Larson's lot. One by one classmates straggled over to the entrance of the cave. Elizabeth counted ten, then twelve, then fifteen

kids. By seven o'clock a crowd of almost twenty was
there. Word had spread about Aaron, and everyone's
curiosity was growing.

"I'll bet he went home," Dennis said, sticking
his head into the cave. "You in there, Dallas? Or did
a ghost get you?"

A few kids laughed nervously, but most just
watched with eager fascination. A minute later,
though it seemed like much longer, Aaron crawled
out of the cave.

"Here I am, Cookman. No ghosts got me, but
I've got to admit it was a little damp in there."

Everyone cheered and started chanting Aaron's
name. Elizabeth leaned over to whisper in Amy's
ear. "He really looks like he spent the night in there.
Whose idea was it to rumple up his clothes and put
mud on his face?"

"Mine," Amy said proudly.

"Aaron!" Jessica screamed, sighing with relief.
"You're a hero!"

But Aaron was busy watching Dennis's reaction.
"It wasn't so bad in there, Dennis. Maybe you
should try it," he said casually.

That was when Ken piped up. "I bet I could do
it, too. I'm going to spend the night in the cave tonight!"

Dennis looked at Ken with disbelief. Ken was a

lot smaller than Aaron and not known for being brave. It was one thing for Aaron to be heroic, but Ken Matthews? Dennis shrugged.

"I'll tell you one thing," he said, "I'm not going to believe *you* spent a whole night in there until we find some people to stay out here all night to guard the entrance."

"Go ahead," Ken said. "You sit up all night and watch the front of the cave, Dennis. I won't come out, I promise you."

Dennis grunted. "Well, I'm not going to do it alone. I want someone to watch with me."

"I will," Aaron said.

Dennis shook his head. "You're too involved already." He narrowed his eyes at Jimmy, who was cowering behind Elizabeth. "How about you, Undersized? Want to spend the night watching the cave with me?"

Aaron nudged Jimmy. "Say yes," he instructed in a whisper.

Jimmy looked like he'd rather die. "Uh . . . yes," he squeaked. "But what am I going to tell my parents?" he demanded.

"Tell them you're sleeping over at my house," Aaron said. "Ken, you can tell your parents the same thing."

"OK," Dennis said in a take-charge voice as he

turned to Ken. "Same rules, right? No flashlight. Just some food and water. You go in at seven. Under-sized and I will sit here and watch the cave till seven tomorrow morning. If you so much as cast a shadow outside that cave, it doesn't count."

"It's a deal," Ken said cheerfully. "Any advice you want to give me?" he asked Aaron.

Aaron fixed his eyes on Dennis as he spoke. "Well, it's pretty scary in there," he said, winking at Ken to signal this was all staged for Dennis's benefit. "I heard some noises that made me think for sure I was a goner. The thing to do is to concentrate on something else. Don't think about where you are. Try to forget you're in Dead Man's Cave."

"I think we'd better take you out for some breakfast," Elizabeth said, linking arms with Aaron and Ken. "That way you can *really* give Ken some good advice."

It took a while for them to extricate themselves from the group, but finally Elizabeth, Amy, Ken, Aaron, and Jimmy were alone together. They stopped at the Dairi Burger for a Sunrise Special breakfast and began to plan the night's strategy.

"I think it went really well. Dennis is definitely getting bugged by the whole thing," Ken said, taking a bite of his French toast.

"Yeah. It was the easiest thing in the world. I

was only in the cave about an hour last night, and then I just cut through the woods out back and raced home."

"Wasn't it terrible . . . even for that hour?" Elizabeth asked.

Aaron shrugged. "It wasn't bad. Besides, it'll be worth it to see how horrified Dennis is when he has to actually spend the whole night in there." He grinned. "Now, Jimmy, you know what the deal is. Tomorrow morning when Ken comes out, it's your turn to volunteer."

Jimmy wasn't touching his breakfast. "You guys seem to be forgetting something. Ken just has to stay in the cave for one hour and then he can go home. What about me?" He shuddered, looking pale. "I've got to spend the whole horrible night sitting in front of Dead Man's Cave with Dennis Cookman!" As if the full horror of it had just hit him, he began to shiver. "I think I'd rather die. I'd rather be inside the cave. I'd rather be anywhere!"

"Be brave, Jimmy," Elizabeth said gently. "Remember, it's for a good cause. Besides, you're the one who knows what's really going on, and Dennis doesn't."

Jimmy's lower lip trembled. He couldn't imagine anything worse in the world than sitting up all night keeping watch over the cave with Dennis. But he could tell he didn't have a choice.

Elizabeth heard voices in the family room when she let herself into the house later that afternoon. One voice sounded very distraught, and the other voice—Jessica's—sounded reassuring. Elizabeth went inside, trying to figure out who had come over.

"Jessica, I just can't go through with it," the girl said. She sounded like she was crying. "You should've seen what happened this morning! I went up to Dennis at Larson's lot and tried to say hi, and he pushed me out of his way like I was . . . I don't know, like dirt. There's no way I'm ever going to get him to agree to have lunch with me."

"Come on, Grace," Jessica said soothingly. "You've done so well. You're almost a Unicorn. I know you can do it. You don't even have to spend the whole lunch hour with him. Just get him to sit down with you and you're through."

Elizabeth froze. She couldn't believe her ears. Jessica was making Grace Oliver convince Dennis Cookman to eat lunch with her?

"I want to be a Unicorn more than anything," Grace said tearfully, "but I think this task is impossible. I'll try, but I just want you to know I don't think I can do it." Elizabeth heard a chair scrape and she scrambled into the other room so the girls wouldn't see her. Her eyes flashed indignantly. So reciting that poem out loud in class wasn't the only thing Grace had to do. Elizabeth never thought Jessica could do something like this. And she intended to tell her exactly how she felt.

As soon as she heard the front door close, Elizabeth stormed back into the family room to confront her twin. "Jessica," she said, crossing her arms and glaring at her, "would you mind telling me what that was all about?"

"What was what all about?" Jessica asked innocently.

"I overheard you and Grace Oliver just now," Elizabeth retorted. "What's the deal? Are you trying to torture her? How can you possibly ask *anyone* to get Dennis Cookman to have lunch with them? It would be easier if you asked her to have lunch with the President! Dennis wouldn't sit down with someone—voluntarily—for a million dollars!"

Jessica shrugged. "It isn't supposed to be easy, Lizzie. If it were, it wouldn't be a very good test, would it? The whole point is to find out whether or not Grace is good material for the Unicorns. If she can't do this, maybe she isn't."

Now Elizabeth was really fuming. "I thought

you gave up initiation rites a long time ago. I don't know what made you bring them back, but if you ask me, you guys are treating Grace horribly. If she's going to be in your club, you ought to treat her with respect—like a friend. Instead you're . . . you're bullying her, just like Dennis bullies Jimmy and the rest of us," she concluded. "You have no right to do this to her. In fact, I think you all owe her a big apology. I'm amazed she still wants to have anything to do with you!" With that Elizabeth stormed out of the room.

Jessica looked after her. She couldn't believe her very own sister had compared her to Dennis Cookman. How could she say that about a few simple initiation rites? Jessica bit her lip. Maybe getting Dennis to eat lunch with her was a little too difficult for Grace. She didn't want to get a reputation for being unfair. She hated to be the one to suggest modifying Grace's last task. But if she had to do it, she might as well get some points for it. If she acted quickly, she could make it seem like she was the one who'd decided they were being too hard on Grace. And then she could be the one to tell Grace they'd decided to let her off easy.

"OK, Undersized," Dennis said, "gimme that flashlight. It's just you and me now. So you'd better do what I say."

Jimmy handed Dennis the flashlight. He couldn't believe it got so dark by eight-thirty. He trembled and glanced over at Dennis.

Dennis was hunched up, his arms around his knees, moving the flashlight around so the light moved up and down in the weeds. Larson's lot was spooky at night. They could hear twigs snap every once in a while and the wind whoosh through the trees behind the cave. It sounded like an army of ghosts on parade.

Jimmy shivered. "It's kind of cold here." He stared uneasily at the cave. "Did you ever . . . have you ever seen a ghost, Dennis?"

Dennis stared at Jimmy. "Nah. I don't believe in ghosts," he said. But his voice didn't sound very steady.

"I guess if I were as big as you, I wouldn't mind so much," Jimmy said, taking a deep breath. A twig snapped close by and Jimmy jumped. "What's that?" he demanded.

"Cut it out, twerp," Dennis said angrily. He glared at Jimmy, who inched away nervously. "Just keep quiet or I'm going to pound you."

Jimmy held his breath. *Great*, he thought. *I don't know which is worse—having to sit here all night waiting for ghosts to crawl out of the cave, or being beaten up by Dennis.* He sure hoped this plan of Aaron's worked.

"We'll just see if that little creep doesn't come crawling out, scared half to death," Dennis said, shining the flashlight on the entrance to the cave.

Jimmy sighed forlornly. Pulling his sweatshirt tightly around him, he stared at the entrance to Dead Man's Cave, praying that morning would hurry up and come.

"Hey!" Dennis's voice cut through the darkness. "What's the matter? You sleeping or something?"

Jimmy opened his eyes with a start. At first he couldn't remember where he was, but the crick in his neck and the sour taste in his mouth reminded him. It was morning! Jimmy scrambled joyfully to his feet.

"Well, I didn't see him come crawling out, did you?" Dennis said doubtfully.

"No," Jimmy said. It was ten minutes to seven.

"You in there, Matthews?" Dennis hollered.

"Where else would I be?" Ken called back in a cheerful voice. "You don't have to shout, Dennis." He peeped out of the front of the cave, giving Jimmy the thumbs-up sign. "Not a bad place to spend the night," he added. "You guys ought to try it. It's much more comfortable in here than out there."

Dennis glared at him. But before he could answer, Aaron hollered from the edge of the lot. The welcoming committee had arrived!

This morning over two dozen kids showed up to see if Ken had made it through the night. All weekend long news of the Dead Man's Cave exploit was spreading, and today a few kids from Sweet Valley High School came, too. Steven arrived with the twins and looked at Ken with disbelief.

"It was nothing," Ken said calmly, stepping out of the cave to loud cheering.

"Well, Cookman?" Aaron asked. "Did you keep an eye on him? Make sure he didn't crawl out during the night?"

Dennis looked with disgust at Jimmy. "Yeah. *I* kept an eye on him," he said. "Someone else fell asleep on the job."

"Who's next?" Ken asked brightly.

Aaron nudged Jimmy, who gave him a pleading look.

"It's really not bad," Ken added. "Come on. Who's going to be the next one to prove Dead Man's Cave isn't such a bad place after all?"

Jimmy took a deep breath. "Uh . . . I will," he said in a quavering voice.

Dennis snorted. "Give me a break," he snarled. "*You* spend the night in there, Undersized?"

Jimmy nodded. "Yeah," he said in a soft voice, "Yeah, me."

Dennis stared at him, the flashlight dangling from his hand. "No way," he said at last. "If you spend the night in there, I'll . . ." His voice trailed off disbelievingly.

This was the moment Aaron had been waiting for. "What will you do?" he asked eagerly. "If Jimmy spends the night in there, are you going to do it the next night?"

Dennis stared at Aaron. There were twenty or thirty kids waiting to hear his reply. "Sure," Dennis said thickly. "Why not? If Undersized can do it, so can I."

Aaron turned to Elizabeth with a triumphant smile. It looked like their plan was working!

Eight

◇

Grace got to school early Monday morning on pur-
pose. She wanted to find Dennis Cookman first
thing so she could ask him to have lunch with her.
Jessica had called her twice at home the night before,
leaving messages, but Grace hadn't called her back.
What was the point? She didn't have any progress to
report, and she didn't want to talk to any of the
Unicorns until she'd convinced Dennis to eat with
her.

Grace had seen Dennis hanging out near the
fence behind the school several mornings the week
before. Now that she'd started looking for him, she
had a sense of where he usually could be found. The

strange thing was that he was always alone, or else he was picking on someone. Grace took a deep breath when she spotted him by the fence. "Dennis!" she called. Then she walked deliberately toward him.

"What do you want?" Dennis asked. It was more a snarl than a question.

Grace summoned up every ounce of courage. "You're going to think this sounds dumb, but I was hoping we could eat lunch together," she said in a soft voice.

"What?" Dennis demanded, obviously astonished.

"I was hoping—"

"I heard you," Dennis interrupted. "What for?"

Grace hadn't thought about this. "Uh . . . I don't know. I just want to," she said lamely.

"Aw, get out of here," Dennis said. He looked embarrassed. He leaned over, picked up a rock, and hurled it as hard as he could into the empty field across from school.

"Does that mean no?" Grace asked, her throat dry.

"Yeah, it means no," Dennis said, not looking at her. Grace felt tears prick behind her eyelids, but she was determined not to show him she was upset. She just shrugged and walked off, trying to seem like it was no big deal. *There goes being a Unicorn*, she thought. And she dragged herself into school.

Jessica, Lila, and Ellen were waiting for her at her locker. "Why didn't you call me back last night? I've been frantic," Jessica announced.

Grace blinked back tears. "I didn't want to admit that I'm a failure. Look, you guys," she said, facing the three girls squarely, "I'm obviously not Unicorn material. I tried my hardest with Dennis, but I can't get him to have lunch. So I guess that's it."

Lila and Ellen exchanged glances.

"Look," Jessica said, her voice full of compassion, "we understand. In fact, I got to thinking about it yesterday after you left, and I decided it was too much to ask of you. You've done a great job on the other parts of the initiation. All you have to do is one more tiny initiation rite, and then you can be a Unicorn. All you have to do is find a purple sweatshirt for every Unicorn. You don't have to buy them. Just scout around and tell us where we can get them. After that, you're in!" Jessica beamed as if she'd just done Grace a great big favor.

Grace stared at her. "Really? You mean it? You mean I can be a Unicorn without getting Dennis to have lunch with me?"

Jessica nodded. She felt like she was the nicest,

most generous person in the whole world, and she was glad Grace seemed to agree. "That's what being a Unicorn is all about," she said triumphantly. "It means being extra-special nice to someone special. We're giving you a break because we really want you to be a Unicorn."

Grace looked positively overjoyed. "I don't know how to thank you . . . " she began.

Jessica waved her hand. "Don't even think about it," she said. She gave Ellen and Lila a triumphant smile. They had warned her that Grace might be angry for having had to go through all the trouble with Dennis, but Jessica knew better. She had known how grateful Grace would be to get to be a Unicorn. Plus, if Grace could find the sweatshirts, they'd all have an excuse to buy something new.

Obviously Jessica had made the right move!

Grace arrived at the lunchroom late and looked around for a place to put her tray. She'd been talking to Mr. Bowman about an essay she had written on *The Adventures of Tom Sawyer*. Now she was so late there was nowhere to sit. At last she sat down at an empty table on the left side of the cafeteria, took out her essay, and began to reread it.

"Hey," a gruff voice said. "You still want to have lunch with me?"

Grace looked up, astonished. There was Dennis standing over her, his lunch bag dangling from his big hand. "Uh . . . sure," she said, gulping. She felt like she'd had the wind knocked out of her.

"I don't know why you do," Dennis continued, sitting down and looking at her sullenly.

Grace put down her essay. "I was just curious about you, that's all," she said, improvising. "I wondered why you never sit with anyone."

"Who am I supposed to sit with?" Dennis growled.

Grace shrugged. "Maybe if you weren't so mean to people they'd sit with you," she suggested. She couldn't believe she was actually saying this to Dennis. Her heart started to pound. What if he hit her or something?

But he just looked at her. "People are mean to me, too," he pointed out. "How would you like being called names just because you're big?"

"Big and mean," Grace corrected him. "No one would call you names if you weren't such a bully."

Dennis thought this over. "So why did you want to eat lunch with me, then, if I'm such a bully?" he demanded.

Good question, Grace thought. She could hardly tell him the truth. "I told you. I just wanted to get to know you a little bit."

"Oh." Dennis took his sandwich out, took a bite, and handed it to Grace. "Want some? It's good. My mom made it."

Grace looked at the sandwich. She knew she'd really hurt his feelings if she said no. "OK," she said, picking it up gingerly and taking a minuscule bite.

Dennis grinned. "You aren't that bad," he said. "It isn't so tough eating lunch with you. Who knows," he added. "I might even do it again one day."

Grace smiled weakly at him. "That's great," she said faintly. She hoped Lila, Jessica, and Ellen were watching, wherever they were. Because after what she had just gone through, Grace was sure she deserved a place in the history books.

Jimmy listened to the last instructions from Aaron and Ken on the way home from school.

"Remember, the flashlight's hidden behind the bend, right before you get to the rain pipe," Ken was saying.

"Don't leave right away. Stay for about an hour, long enough to make sure everyone else has gone," Aaron added. "And whatever you do, be sure to get up early enough to be inside the cave before six-thirty. Dennis will probably get there early tomorrow morning to check."

Jimmy nodded.

"Oh, and don't make any noise when you leave or return. There's a whole bunch of twigs and dry leaves and stuff behind the rain pipe. Be careful not to rustle them."

"OK, OK." Jimmy sighed. "I guess I'm ready."

"You're going to do a great job," Aaron said, slapping him on the back. "We're counting on you. And remember, tomorrow night's the night. Dennis is going to be scared out of his big-bully mind in there!"

"Yeah," Jimmy said hollowly. Aaron and Ken turned right at their block, and Jimmy continued on. "Well, see you tonight, guys."

He was almost home when he heard a voice call him. "Hey, Undersized! Wait up!"

Great, Jimmy thought, *Dennis Cookman. Just what I need to make a rotten day more rotten. Maybe he'll beat me up so I can be in total pain tonight as well as total terror.*

"You really planning on spending the night in that cave?" Dennis demanded, panting a little as he ran to catch up with Jimmy.

Jimmy nodded.

"Well, I wouldn't if I were you. Haven't you heard the stories about the little guy who spent the night in there five years ago?" Dennis grimaced.

"They say there's some kind of curse on the place, and if you get dirt on you from Dead Man's Cave, you die the night before you turn fifteen."

Jimmy took a deep breath. "Well, I guess we're both in for it, then. 'Cause after tonight, it's your turn."

Dennis blinked, and Jimmy walked off, his head held high. He couldn't help feeling like he'd won a small victory. He wasn't going to be scared by a bully, and he wasn't going to get scared that night in the cave, either. He was going to do it, whether or not there were ghosts and curses.

Just a few hours later Jimmy couldn't believe how easy it had been. As soon as everyone else had gone, he scooped up the flashlight, and crawled out through the rain pipe. He climbed easily up the hill into the woods, being careful not to make noise, and was able to slip inside his house just before eight-thirty. He told his mother he'd been over at Ken's house, working on a social studies project. She just smiled at him and nodded. "Don't stay up too late, dear. It's a school night," she warned. Jimmy hid a smile. He intended to go to sleep right away so he'd be able to wake up at five-thirty when his alarm went off. He wanted to be sure everything went smoothly in the morning. The others were counting on him.

It all went without a hitch. The alarm went off, Jimmy sneaked out of the house without making a single noise, and by six-thirty he was safe inside the cave again. He even remembered to rumple his hair and rub some dirt on his face so he would look as if he had spent the entire night there. At seven o'clock he crept out of the cave, where a whole crowd had gathered to see whether he'd made it. Everyone cheered, and Aaron hoisted him up on his shoulders, shouting out his name.

"OK, Dennis," Ken said, crossing his arms. "You're on for tonight, right?"

Dennis wiped his brow, looking nervously around him. "I don't know," he said. "I've got a really bad sore throat. Maybe we should put it off till tomorrow or something."

"Aw, come on, Cookman," Aaron said. "A deal's a deal. You don't want to back down now, do you?"

Dennis swallowed cautiously. "My throat," he said, looking paler by the minute. "You know how stupid it is to sit around in the damp air if you're coming down with something." He didn't meet Aaron's gaze. "I'd better not do it tonight."

Aaron looked disgusted. "You don't have a sore throat!"

"I do, too," Dennis said, sounding offended. "I

told you—I'll do it when I feel better." And with that he stormed off. As everyone watched him go an explosion of name-calling, taunting, and mockery broke out.

"We're not going to let him get away with it," Aaron said grimly. "A deal's a deal. Let's make sure we all give Dennis an extra-hard time in school today. Whatever it takes, we're going to get him in that cave tonight. *All* night."

Everyone cheered. They couldn't wait to see Dennis get a taste of his own medicine. They were going to do everything they possibly could to make sure he got the biggest scare of his life.

Nine
◇

"None of us could believe it when we saw you and Dennis yesterday," Jessica gushed to Grace. "See? You just didn't have enough self-confidence. You made it through the initiation just fine, after all!"

Grace was standing in the corridor on Tuesday morning with Jessica, Lila, and Ellen, proudly wearing the purple shoelaces they had just given her. "Oh, well," she said modestly, "you just never know with these things."

Ellen frowned. "Were you guys at Dead Man's Cave this morning?"

The girls all shook their heads. "I'm getting

tired of that whole cave thing," Jessica complained. "How many people are going to spend the night in there? I think it's dumb."

"Well," Ellen said with a mischievous grin, "I just bumped into Caroline Pearce. She said Jimmy actually managed to stay in there all night. So now Dennis has got to do it."

Jessica looked bored. "So what? If Jimmy can stay in there all night, why can't Dennis?"

"Well, according to Caroline, Dennis is chickening out. He said he was going to do it, but now he says he's got a sore throat."

Everyone laughed. "You mean big brave Dennis is more of a coward than little Jimmy Underwood?" Lila cried.

"Caroline told me that Aaron wants everyone to give Dennis a hard time about it today until he agrees to go in," Ellen said.

Everyone grinned. "You can see why Caroline's such a good one for the job," Ellen concluded.

"Well, maybe this whole thing isn't boring after all," Jessica pronounced, tossing back her hair. "If it's going to make Dennis look like a baby, it might just turn out to be fun." Her eyes sparkled. "We better make it official Unicorn business to bug him today— and to be sure to be at Larson's lot tonight!"

* * *

"Hey, Dennis! What's your problem? Think you're going to see a ghost tonight?" one of the seventh-graders jeered.

Dennis glared at him. The whole morning had been like this, and lunch was even worse. Everyone who saw him said something about the cave.

"How's your throat, Dennis?" Caroline Pearce asked, sailing through the lunch line.

"Kind of surprising," Peter DeHaven said to him with a little smile, "when you figure even Jimmy wasn't afraid to spend the night in the cave . . ."

Dennis paid for his lunch, still fuming. He had just finished putting the change back in his wallet when Lila and her eighth-grade cousin Janet Howell jumped up behind him, screaming, "Boo!"

"Get out of my way!" Dennis growled. But the girls didn't look very frightened.

Grace was sitting by herself in the corner of the lunchroom, putting the finishing touches on the revision of the essay she'd written for Mr. Bowman. She was so deep in thought, she didn't notice Dennis coming over.

"Hey," he said in a gruff voice. "Someone sitting here?"

"Dennis!" Grace exclaimed. "Uh . . . no. Go

right ahead." She felt flustered and confused. Was he going to sit with her every day now? She hoped she wasn't going to have a problem on her hands. Once was OK, but she didn't want him thinking they were best friends now.

Dennis unwrapped his sandwich and offered her half.

"No, thanks," Grace said firmly. "I already ate."

Dennis ate the sandwich in three big bites. "Have you heard the dare about the cave tonight?" he asked mournfully.

"A little bit. I heard you promised to spend the night in there if Jimmy did," Grace said carefully, "and now you say you can't. Is that right?"

Dennis stared at her. "There's no way I can spend the night in that place—tonight," he said. "My throat's absolutely *killing* me."

"Maybe you should be at home in bed," Grace said. It was funny. She didn't feel scared of Dennis anymore. She wondered why.

"I just can't spend the night in there," Dennis repeated. His eyes looked huge and scared at the thought. "What do you think I should do?"

Grace set her essay aside. "I think a deal is a deal," she said. "If you don't do it, you'll never hear the end of it. Look, Dennis, you've been mean to everyone around here. You've scared half our class to death. You've bullied everybody. You can't expect people to be nice and forgive you all of a sudden. If I were you, I'd forget about my sore throat and go ahead and do it. Then I'd apologize to Jimmy and Ken and Aaron and some of the others."

Dennis looked morose. "I thought you were different," he said sullenly, getting to his feet. "I thought you'd understand," he said and stomped off.

Grace let out a little sigh of relief. Deep down she felt sorry for Dennis. She could tell he was scared about the cave. He was probably making up the whole thing about his sore throat. But Grace knew he deserved what he got, after the way he'd treated everyone. Still, when she heard everyone jeering at him, she couldn't help feeling sympathetic.

Dennis had really gotten himself into a jam now. She wondered how he was going to handle it.

"He's going to do it!" Aaron crowed, hurrying over to the group. "Jimmy, you took the flashlight out, right?"

Jimmy nodded.

"Good. And did you remember to drag those branches across the back so there's no way he can see through to the rain pipe?"

"Yup," Jimmy said. He grinned. "He's going to be good and scared. Especially after all the stories he told me about the dirt in there being cursed and everything."

"OK," Aaron said. "I told my parents I'm staying over at Ken's to work on this social studies project. Ken, what did you tell your parents?"

"That I'm staying over at Jimmy's," Ken said promptly.

"And I said I'm staying over at Aaron's," Jimmy said, grinning. "I hope no one's mom calls anyone else's mom tonight."

"They won't." Aaron reached into the pocket of his jacket. "We've got the flashlight. So the three of us are going to keep watch over the cave and make sure Dennis doesn't stick one oversized hand or foot out all night long!"

All five of them cheered. They had been waiting for this moment for a very long time.

"I think a lot of people are going to show up tonight," Elizabeth said. "Everyone really got into it today, giving Dennis a hard time about his sore throat. Now that he's going to go ahead and do it, he's going to have a lot of witnesses."

"Good," Ken said. "That'll just make it worse for him if he decides to chicken out."

"OK, guys," Aaron said. "See you all in front of Dead Man's Cave at quarter to seven!"

The boys took off, and Elizabeth and Amy stood in the hallway, looking at each other.

"Why do I have a bad feeling about this?" Elizabeth asked in a low voice.

Amy was looking out the window with a frown. "It doesn't look very nice out," she said. "Is there supposed to be a storm or something?"

Elizabeth shrugged. She hadn't heard a weather report. And she was trying to figure out why she felt slightly apprehensive about Dennis Cookman and Dead Man's Cave.

By ten minutes to seven a huge crowd had gathered in Larson's lot. Elizabeth couldn't believe how many people had shown up. In addition to most of the sixth-graders, a number of seventh-graders had come. By five minutes to seven Dennis seemed to be the only one who hadn't appeared. Everyone was exchanging anecdotes about Dennis—the various fights he'd gotten in, the trouble he'd made in classes or sports.

"He's late," Aaron said at seven o'clock, frowning at his watch.

Elizabeth zipped up her jacket. The sky was dark and threatening, and a strong breeze rustled through the weeds in the field. "Aaron," she said, "maybe we should call this off till the weather clears."

"Are you kidding? After all this trouble?" Aaron shook his head. "Look, here he comes now!"

A hush fell over the crowd as Dennis appeared at the edge of the lot. He looked like a giant in his worn denim jacket and a pair of dark jeans. Like Elizabeth, he was looking apprehensively at the sky.

"Come on, Cookman! Hurry up!" Aaron called.

Dennis walked slowly and deliberately across the lot until he reached the front of the cave. "Listen," he said, "there's supposed to be a bad storm tonight. None of the rest of you stayed in here when there was a storm. Why should I?"

The response from the crowd was overwhelming. "Scared, Cookman?" one of the seventh-graders jeered. "You afraid of a little rain or something?"

Dennis looked down at the ground. "OK," he said finally. "I'll do it." He looked down at his watch. "See you tomorrow morning." He looked pale, but he stepped inside the cave, and everyone cheered.

A rumble of thunder sounded in the distance, and a couple of kids grabbed their bikes and started off across the lot. "Hurry! It's going to pour!" Caroline called, dashing away through the weeds.

Elizabeth looked uneasily at Amy. "I feel bad, leaving him here during a storm," she whispered.

"Oh, he'll be OK," Amy assured her. "He'll be

inside the cave. Come on, Lizzie. We're going to get soaked if we stand out here much longer." Lightning lit up the sky and a loud crash followed.

"Wow," Jimmy said, looking up at the sky. "We'd better get out of here."

Aaron was standing absolutely still, a look of panic on his face.

"Aaron, what is it?" Elizabeth demanded. The first big raindrops were hitting the ground. It looked like the storm was going to come quicker than they'd expected.

"Remember what I told you about that rain pipe?" Aaron demanded. "Remember I said the water didn't drain the way they planned or something?"

Elizabeth shook her head, confused. The raindrops were getting bigger and bigger, and she shivered. A lot of kids were huddling nearby, uncertain whether to run for shelter or wait out the storm. The sky was very dark now and the trees were pitching wildly in the wind.

"If it rains hard enough, that pipe will fill with water and flood the cave!" Aaron cried, raising his voice over the wind and rain. "Dennis could be in trouble. We're going to have to get him out of there now!"

Elizabeth's heart started to pound. She had completely forgotten about the rain pipe. The thought filled her with terror. Any minute rainwater could start flooding the cave.

Ten

◇

"When I count to three," Aaron shouted urgently, "we're all going to yell his name. OK?"

Everyone held their breath and waited. "One, two, three!" Aaron called. "Den—nis!" everyone called together into the cave.

There was no answer.

"Let's try again," Elizabeth urged. "Deennnnn —nnis!" they screamed at the top of their lungs.

"We're going to have to go in there and get him out," Aaron said grimly. "Ken, come with me."

"Let me come, too," Jimmy said in a brave voice.

"Thanks," Aaron said. "You're pretty tough, you know that?"

Elizabeth and Amy were huddled under Amy's rain poncho. A clap of thunder came closer this time, and suddenly the rain was pouring down in torrents. Elizabeth couldn't remember the last time they'd had a storm so sudden and so violent. Jessica and a few other kids had by now run under a small shed at the edge of the lot.

"Is Dennis going to be all right?" Grace Oliver asked, ducking in under Amy's poncho. Her face was pale and her eyes were wide with fear.

Elizabeth quickly explained about the rain pipe. "We've got to get him out of there right away. Otherwise the cave could flood," she said anxiously.

Grace looked close to tears. "It's all my fault. If I hadn't pushed him, he would never have done it," she moaned.

Elizabeth put her arm around the shivering girl, trying to soothe her. It was clear Grace felt responsible, and nothing she could say would calm her down.

"Hand me the flashlight!" Aaron called, taking the lead as the three boys crawled down into the cave. It was really damp inside and darker than it had been any evening when the boys had been in there. They could hear rain pounding with sharp staccato sounds on the metal rain pipe at the back of the cave.

"Dennis, where are you?" Aaron cried. He swung the flashlight's beam from side to side, but the center of the cave was empty.

"There he is!" Jimmy cried, pointing to the cave's side. A narrow ledge had been formed by the excavation, making a shelf about four feet off the ground. Dennis was crouched on the shelf, hugging himself with terror each time thunder crashed outside.

"Dennis, get down. We've got to get you out of here right now," Aaron said, reaching up to give him a hand.

Dennis glared at them. "Yeah, sure. You're going to convince me to leave so you can all laugh at me—tell me I'm a baby." His eyes flashed. "Forget it. You can't trick me. I'm not leaving until tomorrow morning."

"Dennis, there's a big rain pipe back there!" Aaron said rapidly. "I'm not kidding. We all used it to get out of the cave. It's filling up with water and there could be a flood in here. We've got to get you out of here. It's dangerous!"

"Get lost, creeps," Dennis snarled. "I'm not going to trust you. The minute I walk out of this cave you're going to call me a coward. I know it!"

"I'm going to get help," Jimmy cried, turning and racing out of the cave, leaving Aaron and Ken to try and reason with Dennis.

"He won't believe us! He doesn't trust us!" Jimmy cried to the girls. "And there's water pouring in from the back. You guys, what if he won't come out? What if he drowns?"

Grace grabbed Jimmy's hand. "Let me go in there. Maybe he'll listen to me."

She didn't wait for a response but raced through the rain to the entrance of the cave. It was slippery and muddy and Grace almost fell, but she managed to catch herself. "Dennis!" she cried, groping her way forward in the dark cave. She could hear rain pounding on the rain pipe and water gushing into the cave. There was already so much water, she had to wade to where Ken and Aaron were standing.

"Dennis, you have to listen to them. You have to get out of here. Look at the water!" she cried.

Dennis seemed to snap out of it just then. He stared with horror at the water on the cave floor. "Oh, no!" he cried. "We're trapped! We're going to die!"

"Dennis, stay calm," Ken urged. "We're going to get you out of here if you'll just let us help you. Grab hold of my hand," he instructed.

"Come on, Dennis," Grace urged. "Please!"

Grace's voice seemed to be the only thing Dennis could focus on. He leaned forward, trembling violently, and took Ken's hand.

"OK. We've got you now," Ken said. Aaron took Dennis's other hand and they helped the terrified boy down from the ledge into the rising rainwater.

"Grace, get out of here!" Aaron called. "Run!"

Her chest heaving, Grace turned and ran for the mouth of the cave. The water was up to her knees now and she slipped twice, but finally she made it, pulling herself up with the help of Elizabeth, Peter, Amy, and the others waiting outside. Jimmy put his arms around her, and Grace burst into tears.

"There's so much water in there. It's rising so fast," she sobbed.

"We're going to need help!" Ken gasped, sticking his head out of the cave and pulling himself up to safety. "Dennis is too heavy for Aaron to pull up. We're going to have to make a chain."

Aaron scrambled out of the cave next. "OK, Dennis, we're going to pull you out," he called. He planted his feet on the slippery ground and leaned forward, stretching out his arms. Ken moved behind him and grabbed his waist, and Jimmy got behind Ken. Soon the chain reached almost halfway across Larson's lot.

"You ready, Dennis?" Aaron called.

"Hurry!" Dennis sobbed. "The water's up to my waist!"

"OK," Aaron called back. "When I yell three, pull!"

Everyone strained to hear his voice through the pouring rain. "One," Aaron called, "two, three!"

With that the whole line strained backward. Elizabeth pulled as hard as she possibly could. She didn't realize how scared she had been until she heard Aaron yell, "He's out!" And the next minute everyone tumbled backward with the surprise of letting go.

Dennis flung his arms around Aaron, half-laughing, half-crying. They had saved his life, and for the moment that was all that mattered.

The storm stopped almost as quickly as it had begun, and the kids who had crawled into the shed for protection came out to find out what had happened. Dennis, dripping with water, was looking hard at Aaron.

"So you guys didn't really spend the whole night in the cave, did you?"

Bit by bit the whole truth came out: how Aaron had found out about the secret escape through the rain pipe; how each had pretended to spend the night in the cave; how they had schemed to get Dennis to spend the night there.

"We wanted to get you back for bullying us," Jimmy explained. "We figured it was only fair."

"I guess you were right," Dennis said gruffly. "I've got to admit it was a pretty good trick. You guys sure fooled me."

Jessica stared indignantly at her twin. "You mean you knew about this all along and never told me?"

Elizabeth grinned. "Everyone has to have a secret sometime, Jess. Even a twin."

Dennis cleared his throat. "There's something I want to say. You guys saved my life tonight. You didn't have to. I acted like a dope and I'm sorry." He turned away. "I'm going home now to think a lot of stuff over. I just want you to know I appreciate what you all did for me in there." He coughed and looked at the ground. "Thanks."

Everyone watched him trudge off across the lot, his wet clothes clinging to him.

"Maybe that will be the end of his bullying," Grace said, her voice cracking. She had learned something, too. Maybe it had been unfair of the Unicorns to demand that she get Dennis to have lunch with her. But it had made her do something she would never have done otherwise: she had reached out to someone who was totally alone. She had only done it on a dare, but she'd gained Dennis's trust nonetheless.

Grace felt a little ashamed of herself. She could tell the other Unicorns felt bad, too. Dennis's bullying wasn't a joke and they had made it part of their game.

"I guess it's kind of a lucky thing you got to know Dennis, huh?" Jessica said helpfully, walking home beside Grace.

Grace nodded. "I guess so," she said.

"We think you were awfully brave, Grace," Ellen added. "We're proud that you're a member of the Unicorns."

Grace smiled. "Thanks." She was quiet for a minute. "Listen, I have a request to make. Let's make sure Dennis never finds out the reason I wanted to have lunch with him, OK?"

"Sure," Lila said quickly.

Jessica thought things had worked out pretty well. She was happy that Grace was finally a Unicorn and even happier that Dennis wouldn't be bullying anyone anymore. "Do you suppose he can really be nice?" she asked.

"I wonder if he'll give back my allowance," Lila said.

Jessica pulled her damp hair away from her face

and frowned. There was still one point she thought needed settling, but it would have to wait until she got home.

"I can't believe you never told me about the rain pipe," Jessica said to her twin once they were up in Elizabeth's bedroom with the door closed. When the twins had gotten home, Mrs. Wakefield had sent them both to take hot baths.

Now Elizabeth was drying her hair with a thick towel. "Well, you never told me what you guys put Grace Oliver up to. I had to overhear it. I can't believe you, Jess—making Grace get Dennis Cookman to eat lunch with her."

"It turns out that it was pretty lucky," Jessica said, defending herself.

"I couldn't have told you about the rain pipe even if I'd wanted to. Aaron made us promise not to."

Jessica looked aggravated. "What's the point of being twins if we don't tell each other important things like that?"

Elizabeth laughed. Leave it to Jessica to sound hurt and offended when she herself kept secrets from Elizabeth all the time.

"The important thing is that Dennis is safe—and that he learned his lesson," Elizabeth told her. "I'm sure he'll be much nicer to everyone from now on."

She could hardly wait for school the next day to see whether or not Dennis Cookman would be acting any differently!

"If you'd told me a week ago that Dennis would be eating lunch with Jimmy Underwood instead of eating Jimmy Underwood's lunch, I never would have believed it," Janet Howell remarked.

The Unicorns were in their special corner of the lunchroom, watching Dennis with fascination.

"It's pretty incredible," Lila agreed. Her eyes were shining, and Jessica could tell she was just dying to spring some kind of big secret on the group. "So hasn't anyone heard the news yet?" she said finally.

"What news?" Jessica demanded. She hated to think Lila knew something she didn't know.

Lila took a deep breath. "Now, don't all start screaming when I tell you this," she said. "You know Kent Kellerman, the gorgeous guy who plays Neil on *All the World*?"

All the World was the Unicorn Club's favorite soap opera. They watched it whenever they could and made sure to videotape it when they were at school so they never missed a single episode. And Neil was most of the reason.

"Which one is Neil?" Grace asked innocently.

Everyone gasped. "Which one?" Lila repeated, shocked that Grace didn't know.

"He's the star," Janet said reprovingly. "At least, he's the star since Phillip got shot and Tex moved away and Tyrone turned out to be a criminal."

"Oh," Grace said. "You mean the rich guy who wears dark suits and is in love with the blond woman who just had an eye operation?"

"No!" Jessica cried, anguished. "He's the juvenile delinquent who just moved from the East—at least everyone *thinks* he's a juvenile delinquent, but really he's the son of Seville Lyons, that guy who was on last year for a few months who was married to Noelle's mother."

"Oh," Grace said, still confused. "I think I know which one he is."

No one else was one bit in doubt. Neil was their new hero, and nearly every member of the club had a picture of Kent Kellerman taped inside her locker or over her bed.

"Anyway, what about Kent, Lila?" Jessica prompted.

"You're going to die. Absolutely die. Daddy has a friend in Hollywood who works with one of the producers of *All the World*. Apparently they're doing a special on-location episode right here in Sweet Valley. And Kent Kellerman is going to be the major actor in the scene!"

Forgetting their promise to be silent, everyone started to shriek. Jessica couldn't believe her ears. Kent Kellerman coming to Sweet Valley? It was unbelievable.

"Look, I've got it all written down," Lila said triumphantly. "Mr. Kellerman will arrive at nine o'clock on Monday. Scenes will be shot at Chester Street, Main Street, the Valley Mall, and the Cinema."

Everyone was frantic with excitement. "We're going to get to see Kent Kellerman in person!" Jessica cried, her eyes sparkling with excitement. "You guys, what on earth am I going to wear?"

Janet looked stricken. "You're right," she moaned. "We're going to have to think of something. We can't all wear purple sweatshirts to meet Kent Kellerman."

"Aren't you all forgetting something?" Grace asked, looking at her calendar.

"What? Forgetting what?" Lila demanded, turning to her with a frown.

"You said he's coming on a Monday," Grace said calmly. "How are we going to see Kent Kellerman if we're supposed to be in school?"

Everyone looked at Grace as if she had dropped

a bomb in the middle of the table. She was right. The shrieks of joy faded to a stunned, miserable silence.

Kent Kellerman was coming to Sweet Valley. And it looked as if the Unicorns were going to be stuck in school the whole time he was there!

Will Jessica and Lila find a way to meet Kent Kellerman? Find out in Sweet Valley Twins #20, **PLAYING HOOKY.**

Join Jessica and Elizabeth for an exciting adventure in Sweet Valley Twins Super Edition #1, **THE CLASS TRIP.**

IT ALL STARTED WITH

THE
SWEET
VALLEY
TWINS

For two years teenagers across the U.S. have been reading about Jessica and Elizabeth Wakefield and their High School friends in SWEET VALLEY HIGH books. Now in books created especially for you, author Francine Pascal introduces you to Jessica and Elizabeth when they were 12, facing the same problems with their folks and friends that you do.

☐ BEST FRIENDS #1   15421/$2.50
☐ TEACHER'S PET #2   15422/$2.50
☐ THE HAUNTED HOUSE #3   15446/$2.50
☐ CHOOSING SIDES #4   15459/$2.50
☐ SNEAKING OUT #5   15474/$2.50
☐ THE NEW GIRL #6   15475/$2.50
☐ THREE'S A CROWD #7   15500/$2.50
☐ FIRST PLACE #8   15510/$2.50
☐ AGAINST THE RULES #9   15518/$2.50
☐ ONE OF THE GANG #10   15531/$2.50
☐ BURIED TREASURE #11   15533/$2.50
☐ KEEPING SECRETS #12   15538/$2.50
☐ STRETCHING THE TRUTH #13   15554/$2.50
☐ TUG OF WAR #14   15550/$2.50
☐ THE OLDER BOY #15   15556/$2.50
☐ SECOND BEST #16   15563/$2.50
☐ BOYS AGAINST GIRLS #17   15571/$2.50
☐ CENTER OF ATTENTION #18   15581/$2.50

Get Ready for a Thrilling Time in Sweet Valley®!

☐ **26905 DOUBLE JEOPARDY #1**   **$2.95**

When the twins get part-time jobs on the Sweet Valley newspaper, they're in for some chilling turn of events. The "scoops" Jessica invents to impress a college reporter turn into the real thing when she witnesses an actual crime—but now no one will believe her! The criminal has seen her car, and now he's going after Elizabeth . . . the twins have faced danger and adventure before . . . but never like this!

Watch for the second Sweet Valley Thriller Coming in May

Prices and availability subject to change without notice.

Buy them at your local bookstore or use this handy coupon for ordering: